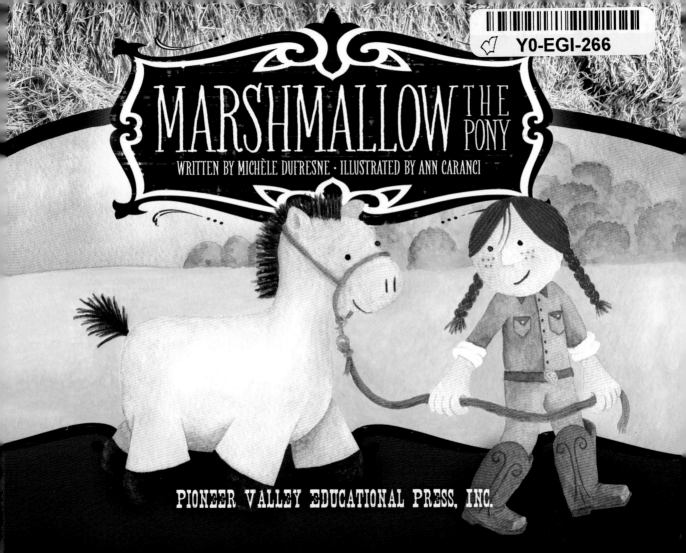

MARSHMALLOW THE PONY

WRITTEN BY MICHÈLE DUFRESNE · ILLUSTRATED BY ANN CARANCI

PIONEER VALLEY EDUCATIONAL PRESS, INC.

I feed my pony.

3

I walk my pony.

I ride my pony.

I wash my pony.

9

I comb my pony.

I brush my pony.

I kiss my pony.

15

I clean my pony's barn.

Y0-DYL-650

JAN 9   1996

The
Shih Tzu

by William R. Sanford
and Carl R. Green

CRESTWOOD HOUSE

New York

CIP
LIBRARY OF CONGRESS CATALOGING IN PUBLICATION DATA

Sanford, William R. (William Reynolds)
  Shih tzu

  (Top dog)
  Includes index.
  SUMMARY: Discusses the history, physical characteristics, care, and breeding of the
dog which descended from the lion dogs of old China.
  1. Shih tzu — Juvenile literature. [1. Shih tzu. 2. Dogs.] I. Green, Carl R. II. Title.
III. Series: Sanford, William R. (William Reynolds), Top dog.
SF429.S64S26   1989   636.7'6 — dc20   89-31108
ISBN 0-89686-448-0

▌PHOTO CREDITS

Cover: Photo Researchers, Inc.: Toni Angermayer
Photo Researchers, Inc.: (Toni Angermayer) 14, 39
Animals Animals: (Robert Pearcy) 4; (Jerry Cooke) 16; (Mike & Moppet Reed)
    21, 26
Betty Meidlinger: 9, 13, 29, 37
Helen Mueller: 10, 23, 32, 42

Macmillan Publishing Company
866 Third Avenue
New York, NY 10022
Collier Macmillan Canada, Inc.

CRESTWOOD HOUSE

Produced by Carnival Enterprises

Printed in the United States of America

First Edition

10   9   8   7   6   5   4   3   2   1

TABLE OF CONTENTS

FOR MORE INFORMATION

For more information about Shih Tzus, write to:

American Kennel Club
51 Madison Avenue
New York, NY 10010

American Shih Tzu Club, Inc.
P.O. Box 431469
Miami, FL 33243

THE "LION DOG"

Grandfather Ben smiled as he watched Scott playing with Drin. As the Shih Tzu sat up and saluted, Scott threw him a biscuit. Then he picked up the dog and gave him a hug.

Scott turned to his grandfather. "I think Exalted Mandarin Warrior is tired out," he said. "Of course, if I was a small dog with a name that long, I'd be tired, too. Isn't that right, Drin?" Two bright eyes looked fondly at the boy from beneath a fringe of silver hair.

"Now, Grandfather, tell me again about China and Great-Grandfather's first Shih Tzu," Scott went on. He said the name of the breed the way Ben had taught him: *Shid Zoo*.

Ben Parker knew Scott never tired of hearing the old story. "You remember," he said, "that my father was a missionary in China. That was a long time ago, in 1908, to be exact. His mission school was in Beijing, the capital city."

Scott pulled a stool close to Ben. Drin dozed in his arms.

"That year, everyone in Beijing was worried about the health of Tzu-hsi, the dowager em-

For many years small, silky Shih Tzus were only seen in Chinese palaces.

5

press. She was very sick. Then, word came that the Dalai Lama was coming to visit the empress. The Buddhist high priest seldom left Tibet, so this was a great occasion."

"Did Great-Grandfather ever see the empress?" Scott asked.

"No, she lived behind high palace walls," Ben said. "Very few people ever saw her. The story was that she spent much of her time with her tiny dogs. One breed was named 'Pekingese' after Peking — the old name for Beijing. Finally there was the long-haired Shih Tzu."

"I bet the Shih Tzus were her favorites," Scott said.

"That may well have been," Ben agreed. "Then, one day, my father heard that the Dalai Lama had arrived. The best news was that he had given several of his own Shih Tzu Kous to the empress. *Shih tzu* means 'lion,' and *kou* means 'dog.' In those days, the dogs were clipped so that they looked like tiny lions."

"I bet everyone wanted a Shih Tzu after that," Scott said.

"Some rich Chinese asked court servants to steal dogs for them," Ben said. "The servants wouldn't do it. They knew that whoever stole a Shih Tzu *puppy* would be put to death!

"The Chinese found it harder to turn down

requests from Europeans," Ben went on. "A few puppies were sold, but they always died. The story was that the Chinese fed ground glass to the puppies before selling them. That way, they could be sure that the breed would never leave China."

"Well, if that story's true, how did Great-Grandfather come to have a Shih Tzu?" Scott asked.

"After the empress died, the rules were relaxed," Ben explained. "As luck would have it, my father made friends with an official from the palace. It was this man who gave a Shih Tzu puppy to my father. Celestial Dream lived at the mission for many years. She was just as brave and loving as your Drin."

"That's a great story, Grandfather," Scott said. "Now tell me all the other interesting facts about Shih Tzus."

HISTORY OF THE SHIH TZU

Because Shih Tzus are so small, people sometimes forget they're dogs. To understand the breed, remember that Shih Tzus are meat-eating mammals of the scientific order *Car-*

nivora. Their closest relatives come from the family *Canidae.* That means a tiny, long-haired Shih Tzu is kin to wolves, foxes, and jackals. All domestic dogs, from the Shih Tzu to the Saint Bernard, are known by the same species name, *Canis familiaris.*

Today's Shih Tzu is descended from the lion dogs of old China. Beyond that, the story of these small, silky lapdogs is hard to trace. One theory says the dogs were first imported from Turkey about 1,300 years ago. At first, they were known as *Fu Lin,* the Chinese name for Turkey. By the 1800s, the name of lion dog— *Shih Tzu* in Chinese—was in common use.

A more popular theory names Tibet as the birthplace of the Shih Tzu. Hidden deep in the Himalaya Mountains, Tibet was a remote land ruled by Buddhist monks. Along with their religious duties, the monks bred fine dogs. They developed the chow chow, the Tibetan mastiff, the Tibetan terrier, and the Lhasa Apso. Their favorite, however, was the lion dog.

This tiny dog was named for the snow lion, because it looked like this mythical beast. The Shih Tzu was also related to the god of learning. This god took the form of a lion with the Buddha riding on its back. The lion was so powerful that when it roared, seven dragons fell out of the sky! Another story claims that

8

Today's Shih Tzus are related to the "lion dog" found in old China.

wicked monks were sometimes reborn as Shih Tzus.

Tibet's chief priest, the Dalai Lama, gave some of his precious Shih Tzus to China's rulers. The last gift came in 1908, the year the dowager empress died. After her death, China was torn apart by revolution. The empress's Forbidden Palace was thrown open and a new government took over. For the first time, it was possible for Westerners to have Shih Tzus.

In the 1930s, a British general took a pair of Shih Tzus back to England. At first, the dogs

In 1969, the American Kennel Club accepted Shih Tzus as a separate breed. Since then, these lapdogs have won many show awards.

were known as Tibetan lion dogs. That changed in 1934, when the name Shih Tzu came into general use. By 1955, over 500 Shih Tzus were registered with the British Kennel Club. Shih Tzus also showed up in Canada, Norway, Australia, and other countries.

The Shih Tzu was little known in the United States before the 1940s. After World War II, members of the armed forces brought Shih Tzus home with them. To their dismay, the breed wasn't accepted by the American Kennel Club (AKC). In self-defense, Shih Tzu owners formed the American Shih Tzu Club in 1963. Finally, in March 1969, the AKC accepted Shih Tzus as a separate breed. As if to celebrate, a Shih Tzu named Ying Ying won top honors at a New Jersey show that same year. Ying Ying beat out 970 other dogs to carry off Best in Show honors.

Since then, Shih Tzus have become the most popular of all the toy breeds. They outsell Yorkshire terriers, Chihuahuas, and other lapdogs. One look at a Shih Tzu will tell you why.

A CLOSE-UP OF THE SHIH TZU

Most Shih Tzu owners think their pets are the most beautiful dogs in the world. In the 1930s, the members of the Peking Kennel Club thought so, too. The club's standards for the lion dog stated: "It should have the head of a lion, the torso of a bear, and the hoof of a camel." In addition, the dog must have "a feather-duster tail, palm-leaf ears, teeth like grains of rice, a pearly petal tongue, and the movements of a goldfish."

Show-quality Shih Tzus do display these

qualities. They have large heads, sturdy bodies, and long, silky coats. These small, graceful dogs have perfectly formed ears and tails. Owners don't like to call them toys, because the name suggests that the breed is delicate. When you pick up a Shih Tzu, you'll discover it's as solid as a small bear. Nevertheless, the AKC puts Shih Tzus in the "toy group" at its dog shows.

Shih Tzus vary greatly in size. Adult dogs range from 8 to 11 inches in height (measured at the shoulder, or *withers*). Ten inches is said to be ideal. A show-quality Shih Tzu's body should be longer than its height. Weights vary from 9 to 18 pounds. The ideal range is from 12 to 15 pounds.

The Shih Tzu's head is broad and round. The round, dark eyes are set wide apart. The muzzle is quite short, but not flattened. From the tip of the nose to the base of the dog's forehead is only about an inch. A shock of hair falls over the eyes, and Shih Tzus have long beards and whiskers. This halo of hair, some people say, makes them look like chrysanthemums. To complete the picture, Shih Tzus have long, drooping ears. The hair on the ears often blends with the long hair of the neck.

A number of colors in the Shih Tzu are ac-

12 *Show-quality Shih Tzus have round heads, sturdy bodies, and long, silky coats.*

The color of a Shih Tzu's coat can range from gold to silver to bright apricot.

ceptable to breeders. Shades of gold, from light to dark, are quite common. Even solid gold dogs often have a black mask and ear fringes. Other desirable colors range from silver to bright apricot. Black-and-white dogs are quite rare. Whatever its color, the coat of a well-groomed Shih Tzu is long and thick. The hair should not be curly, nor should it drag on the ground.

The Shih Tzu's lower jaw often sticks out past the upper jaw. This is known as an *undershot jaw*. The squared-off front of each jaw holds six *incisors* (biting teeth) and two *canines* (tearing or holding teeth). The Shih Tzu also has a full set of 26 *molars* and *premolars* (slicing and crushing teeth). The adult teeth sometimes grow crookedly because there isn't enough room in the dog's small jaw.

A Shih Tzu may look dainty, but it devours its food as if it were still a wild animal. As soon as the chunks are small enough to swallow, down they go! Digestion starts in the stomach, but the final stages of turning food into energy take place in the small intestine. Many of the products of digestion pass through the dog's large liver. This important organ produces bile, needed for digesting a dog's high-fat diet. It also processes the chemicals needed for growth and the repair of body cells.

If you watch a Shih Tzu, you'll see that it

This rare black-and-white Shih Tzu is being investigated carefully by a curious friend.

walks proudly. Perhaps it remembers its noble ancestry. Lively and alert, the dog walks with its head up and its plumed tail arched over its back. Under its lovely coat lies a broad, deep chest and short, muscular legs. The thick coat of hair makes the dog's legs and feet appear even larger than they are. Because of its short legs, the Shih Tzu rolls slightly from side to side as it trots toward you. Overall, the *gait* is smooth and flowing. One poet compared the Shih Tzu in motion to a ship under full sail.

THE SHIH TZU'S KEEN SENSES

The Tibetans used to say that Shih Tzus were next to humans on the ladder of life. Certainly, these dogs are excellent pets—clever and friendly. They adapt quickly to life with their human family. Just don't expect them to do your math homework!

The limits to a dog's thinking abilities are easy to see. Your brain weighs about three pounds. If you weigh 100 pounds, that's 3 percent of your body weight. A ten-pound Shih Tzu's brain weighs about two ounces. Its small brain, therefore, makes up only 1.2 percent of the dog's weight. Most of the dog's brain is occupied with seeing, hearing, and smelling.

The Shih Tzu's eyes are often hidden behind a heavy fringe of hair. Some owners keep the hair out of the eyes by tying it back with a pretty bow. Although their eyes are similar in structure to human eyes, Shih Tzus don't see the world as people do. Dogs are colorblind, and their close vision is poor. They make up for that with good distance vision and excellent night vision. A third eyelid, called the *haw*, closes when the eye is in danger.

Dogs react mostly to movement. If you take a Shih Tzu for a walk on a windless day, it may overlook the neighbor's sleeping cat. The dog sees only a vague, motionless bump in the driveway. Suddenly, the cat wakes up and runs toward the house. One look at that moving shape spells C-A-T! Only a firm hold on the leash will keep the Shih Tzu from giving chase.

If you can locate one, test your Shih Tzu's hearing with a silent dog whistle. When you blow, you won't hear a thing. Your dog will, and it will respond at once. The reason is simple. The human ear cannot hear high-pitched tones above 20,000 cycles a second. A dog's ears pick up sounds as high as 40,000 cycles a second. A Shih Tzu also hears fainter sounds than you can, and it's better at locating the source of a sound. After all, the dog has bigger ears than you do, and it can move them without moving its head.

Of all its senses, the Shih Tzu's sense of smell may be the sharpest. The fox, another canidae, depends on its nose to find food and to identify other animals. Dogs carry on this old *instinct*. Inside the Shih Tzu's nose are large *olfactory patches*. When the dog sniffs, molecules in the air register as scents. In one test, six men all picked up stones and threw them. After sniffing each man's hand, a dog easily found the stone he had thrown. Experts guess the dog's sense of smell is at least a million times sharper than yours.

Dogs do have the senses of taste and touch, but they're not as important. Your Shih Tzu can taste sour, sweet, and salty flavors. Even when it's gulping its dinner, it will spit out any food that doesn't taste right. In terms of touch, a dog responds to any pressure against its coat. When you stroke and pet a Shih Tzu, it must feel wonderful.

A SMALL DOG WITH A BIG PERSONALITY

The Shih Tzu is a "people dog." Perhaps, some owners say, that's because Shih Tzus think they're human beings. After all, they've been kept as members of the family for hundreds of years. Luckily, they seem to have forgotten they once were holy dogs who could do no wrong. Today's Shih Tzu is always trying to please you. Try playing fetch-the-stick with another dog. Your Shih Tzu will pick up the game just by watching.

Unlike many small breeds, the Shih Tzu adjusts well to outsiders. With small children, the dog is patient, friendly, and protective. Rowdy children can hurt a small dog, so adults should be ready to step in when things get too rough. Similarly, Shih Tzus accept strangers easily, but they must be properly introduced. Strange dogs are another matter. Even though the other dog is larger, the Shih Tzu will stand its ground. As a result, someone may have to rescue the brave lion dog.

Shih Tzus aren't really lapdogs, but they do like to be picked up and petted. As long as you're sitting quietly, your pet will be content to lie in your lap. When you get up, it will often take over your chair. Shih Tzus clearly prefer to be up where they can see what's happening. Owners swear their dogs think tables are put by windows just so they can look out. Put down on the floor, a Shih Tzu can stage quite a show. These world-class clowns quickly learn the rules of tag, chase-the-ball, and other games. They'll play until their human friends are ready to drop.

Having a dog that's tuned in to people means giving it plenty of attention. If Shih Tzus receive lots of petting, *grooming,* and ex-

20 *Shih Tzu owners know their dogs can quickly learn all kinds of games. This Shih Tzu has learned how to sit up and beg.*

ercise, they're a happy breed. Left alone while humans are at work, they may fill the empty time by chewing on the furniture. Their long hair will mat and tangle if it isn't brushed. Experts say the short-haired breeds are better for people who don't have the time to groom a Shih Tzu.

Exercising a Shih Tzu is easy and fun. A natural house dog, the breed adapts easily to city life. A brisk walk in the park takes care of a day's exercise. In the country, Shih Tzus love to run with horses and to explore the woods and fields. They're good swimmers, but this habit can be dangerous. If a Shih Tzu falls into a stream or river, it may be swept away by the current.

The Shih Tzu's list of good qualities goes on and on. For the most part, it isn't a noisy dog. Instead of yapping, your dog will "talk" to you in a throaty gurgle. The Shih Tzu is seldom shy, and it remains youthful and obedient into old age.

Some owners claim their Shih Tzus smile at them. Hold out a bit of biscuit to a Shih Tzu. It will show its teeth in what might be a grin! It's little wonder their masters are among the happiest of all dog owners.

This Shih Tzu, on the right, looks like he's laughing at something. Some Shih Tzu owners claim their dogs smile at them!

HOW TO CHOOSE A PUPPY

Falling in love with a Shih Tzu is easy. Now, how can you be sure that the puppy you choose will be the right dog for you? Here are some rules to follow.

Rule 1: Buy from a good breeder or pet store. Honest breeders and pet-store owners guarantee their dogs. They won't sell you a puppy

that's ill or one that doesn't like people. You can find Shih Tzus by looking in dog magazines or by asking your local *veterinarian* to help. If you buy from a breeder, you'll be able to pick from a number of puppies. Pet stores are easier to find, but most will have only one or two puppies to show you.

Rule 2: Know what to look for in a healthy puppy. At first glance, all Shih Tzu puppies are wonderful. The differences show up after you watch them a while. Look for a puppy that's carefree and cheerful. Pick it up. Does it feel solid and strong? Are the eyes bright and clear? Are the nose and ears clean? A healthy puppy will smell good when you put your nose against its fur. The seller should give you the puppy's health record, including a list of its shots. Find out if the puppy's parents were checked for *renal dysplasia*. This fatal kidney disease can be a problem in Shih Tzus. Once you buy your puppy, take it to a vet. If it fails the checkup, return it at once.

Rule 3: Quality show dogs cost more. It's exciting to show your Shih Tzu, but a quality *show dog* costs more. It also requires extra care. If you want a show dog, study the standards for the breed. A small problem such as crooked teeth can cost you the blue ribbon. If possible, ask a Shih Tzu expert to help you make your choice. Show dogs start at $500 and go up from there. By contrast, pet-quality dogs cost from $250 to $350. Remember, a pet-quality Shih Tzu is not second best! You're still buying all the love and fun anyone could want.

Rule 4: Register your purebred puppy. People buy purebred puppies because they carry on the qualities of their breed. Your puppy should come with its own *pedigree*. This record lists the dog's ancestors and allows you to register it with a national kennel club. This protects the dog's value if you decide to breed or show your Shih Tzu.

Rule 5: Males are cheaper; females have puppies. Male and female Shih Tzus make equally good pets. If you want a watchdog, buy the more aggressive male. In addition, males are usually a little cheaper to buy. Females are more docile and easier to *housebreak.* If you want to raise puppies, you must have a female. Twice a year your female will come into *heat.* This is when she's ready to mate and have puppies. Stay alert! All the male dogs in the neighborhood will want to visit her.

Rule 6: Make sure the puppy is ready to leave its mother. Puppies should never be sold before they're seven weeks old. Some experts say you should wait until the Shih Tzu is three

or four months old before you buy it. By then, the dog's adult looks and personality will show more clearly. Also, the breeder will have *wormed* the dog and given it the usual puppy shots. Training can start as soon as you take your Shih Tzu home.

A TRAINING COURSE FOR YOUR SHIH TZU

Some Shih Tzu owners start out with the idea that training a small dog will be easy. Little do they know! Like all dogs, Shih Tzus have minds and wills of their own.

The reason for this lies in the difference between humans and dogs. Dogs are creatures of instinct. You can't win an argument with a puppy by reasoning with it. Your Shih Tzu was born with the basic instincts of a wild pack animal. Your job is to use those instincts, not to change them.

Here's how it works. Imagine you've just brought Quang home with you. The fluffy, golden puppy is truly adorable. Right from the start, you give him a sleeping place that's all

Shih Tzu owners can begin training their dogs as soon as they bring them home. But, like all dogs, Shih Tzus have a mind of their own. Shih Tzu owners must be patient and consistent.

his own. A good method is to fix up a bed in a small wooden crate. Lay out some newspapers and an old blanket and the bed is ready. This crate is Quang's den, the place where he feels safest. It's also the place to put him when you don't want him underfoot. That may sound cruel, but leaving a puppy loose leads only to disaster.

The crate gives you a starting place for housebreaking Quang. Like all pack animals, he won't want to soil his own den. You'll notice he's most likely to relieve himself after he eats and when he wakes from a nap. Those are the times to take him to the place you've chosen. In an apartment, you may want to "paper train" him. Lead him to the newspaper and wait until he uses it. Then praise him warmly. This is known as *reinforcement.* Leave a slightly soiled paper there for the next time. The scent will help in training Quang to this spot. Don't leave other newspapers on the floor. Quang won't know one paper from another!

Each time Quang does well, praise him and pet him. If he makes a mistake, *always* scold him. He will soon accept you as the dominant "dog" of his pack. As the underdog, he'll work hard to please you. The same principle applies to teaching him to come when he's called. If

Most Shih Tzus will want to climb all over the furniture.
Owners must use a firm "No" to keep them off.

you always use his name when you speak to him, he'll learn it quickly. Then, always use the same command: "Come, Quang!" Never take no for an answer. If Quang learns he can ignore your commands, you've lost the battle. He may decide he's top dog, and he'll do whatever he pleases.

The battle of the furniture is next. Quang will want to jump up on every chair, sofa, bed, and table in the house. Give him his own place in each room where he's allowed to stay. Then, use a firm "No, Quang!" when he jumps up.

Whack the floor with a rolled-up newspaper to drive home your point. Do this every time he jumps up. The effort will pay off.

As a house dog, Quang will need a daily walk. For his safety, he must be on a leash. Dog trainers suggest you train him to the leash with a *choke chain*. If Quang tries to run off, pull on the chain. The metal links will cut off his air until he backs down. When he does, release the pressure and praise him. Reinforce the good behavior with a tidbit. In a few days, Quang will be trotting obediently at your heels.

CARING FOR YOUR SHIH TZU

Shih Tzus appear to be small and delicate. In fact, they're quite hardy. You'll find that a Shih Tzu is easy to care for if you follow a few basic rules.

Like all dogs, Shih Tzus need a well-balanced diet. Some owners prepare their dogs' meals "from scratch," while others use a prepared dog food. Whichever you choose, a two-month-old puppy should have five meals a day of milk and ground meat. At four months, you can cut down to three meals. Add cereal, cooked vegetables, and cod-liver oil to the ground meat. By nine months, the Shih Tzu will be close to its adult weight, and you can cut the feedings to two a day. At one year, the dog is no longer a puppy. A single daily feeding will be all it needs.

The most common fault in feeding a Shih Tzu is to give the dog "whatever it wants." That's risky in many ways. Chicken and fish bones can stick in the dog's throat and choke it to death. Sweets cause cavities and leave the dog with a poor appetite for proper foods. Feeding from the table leads to begging and weight gain. Like humans, overweight dogs must be put on diets. Cutting down on meat during hot weather may keep a dog's skin from becoming itchy and irritated. Whatever the diet, a Shih Tzu needs fresh water at least three times a day.

Most Shih Tzus love to be picked up and cuddled. Because of their loose skin, people are tempted to pick them up by the scruff of the neck. That type of lift is painful to the dog. The proper way to pick up a Shih Tzu is to place one hand under the lower chest (the *brisket*) and the other under the rump. As you gather the dog into your arms, support its en-

Shih Tzus need a daily grooming to get rid of burrs and tangles in their coats.

tire body. A fall from four feet can cause a broken bone.

Another important part of caring for a Shih Tzu is its daily grooming. Fifteen minutes a day should be enough to give you a well-groomed, odor-free dog. Brushing stimulates the skin and removes burrs and tangles. When you finish, your dog's hair will shine with glowing good health. If you forget this daily grooming, the heavy hair will soon become matted. At that point, you may have to clip the hair and let it grow in again. If you plan to show the dog, never cut the long hair that grows around the Shih Tzu's face. Tying up the topknot with a bow will keep the hair out of the dog's eyes.

As healthy as they are, Shih Tzus do have some health problems. Long-haired dogs often develop an ear infection called *canker*. Wax also builds up in their ears. For this or a serious problem like worms, take your Shih Tzu to a veterinarian. You'll know the dog has worms if it develops a potbelly, vomits, or has runny eyes. In addition, the vet will keep the dog's shot record up to date and check for kidney problems. You can treat fleas with powder and a flea collar.

The last rule of caring for a Shih Tzu is the most important: Have fun with your dog! Go for walks, play games, hold it in your lap while you're reading. There's no better companion than a well-cared-for Shih Tzu.

BECOMING A SHIH TZU BREEDER

Breeding Shih Tzu puppies seems like the most natural thing in the world. You look at your wonderful 10-month-old Shu-Shu. What a fine mother she'd make! To make it even better, your neighbors have a male who won first place in a local dog show. Why not mate Shu-Shu with Bingo?

Before you breed a Shih Tzu, there are some things to consider. First, think about the age and health of your dog. At her age, Shu-Shu isn't ready for motherhood. Wait until your *bitch* (a female dog) is at least one year old before she has her first *litter*. Next, think about what's best for the breed. Perhaps Bingo is an aggressive, badly spoiled dog. You don't want your puppies to be carbon copies of a bad-tempered male.

After thinking it over, you decide not to use Bingo as Shu-Shu's *stud male*. To find a good stud, ask your vet for the names of some Shih Tzu breeders. Most breeders will have a champion male that you can mate to Shu-Shu. Take the time to meet the breeder and to visit the kennel. Make sure the stud has the qualities you want to see in your puppies. At the same time, the breeder may want to see Shu-Shu. The rule of breeding is a simple one: The better the parents, the better the puppies.

The Shih Tzu's popularity worries the good breeders. Almost any Shih Tzu puppy can be sold for a high price. As a result, careless people are breeding Shih Tzus that shouldn't be mated. This could lower the standards of the breeding stock.

You know, however, that Shu-Shu will have fine puppies. Your next step in breeding is to wait until she comes into heat. When she does, take her to the stud male as close to the thirteenth day as possible. Shu-Shu will probably become pregnant after this first mating. If not, the owner of the stud will tell you to bring her back when she comes into heat again.

Mating your dog to a breeder's male will cost you a stud fee. The most common way to pay is to give the breeder "the pick of the litter." This means you'll have to give up the best puppy that Shu-Shu produces. Because Shih Tzus have small litters, however, you may not want to give up a puppy. In that case, pay the fee in cash.

Shu-Shu will be in heat for several days after you mate her to the stud. Keep her away from other males during that time. If she meets up with an eager terrier, she may give birth to a mixed litter. As the days go by, you'll see that Shu-Shu's body is getting heavier. That means she's pregnant, and it's time to take her to the vet. The vet will give her a checkup, along with some advice on how to care for her. He'll tell you to add protein, eggs, and a little milk to her diet. Exercise Shu-Shu gently, and omit any jumping games while she's carrying her puppies.

You now have less than nine weeks to get ready. Use the time to fix up a *whelping* box (for the birth) and to learn about caring for newborn puppies. Luckily, you can trust Shu-Shu's instincts. Unless a serious problem develops, the birth should go like clockwork.

THE BIRTH OF A SHIH TZU LITTER

Shu-Shu has been carrying her unborn puppies for almost nine weeks. You've given her plenty of good food, exercise, grooming, and love. The vet checked her one last time and clipped the hair around her rump. For the last few nights, Shu-Shu has been sleeping in her whelping box. That's a wise move. Otherwise, she might decide to have her puppies under your bed.

As often happens, the births begin at night. Shu-Shu doesn't seem to need your help. The

When Shih Tzu puppies are ten days old, they open their eyes. A few days later, they are able to stand and walk.

newborn puppy emerges headfirst, covered in its birth sac. Shu-Shu helps the puppy out of the sac and licks it to help it start breathing. She tries to bite off the *umbilical cord,* but her short muzzle keeps her from getting the job done. Now you are needed. You pick up the puppy and cut the cord about one-half inch from the tiny body. Use scissors with rounded tips so you won't injure the puppy.

The pups appear about 30 minutes apart. Shu-Shu licks each blind, deaf pup to clean, warm, and comfort it. Give each puppy a chance to nurse for a few minutes, then move it to a warm basket. You don't want Shu-Shu to sit on it while she's giving birth to the next puppy. Give Shu-Shu some warm milk to drink between births. When the last puppy is born, count the litter. Shu-Shu's litter is a little above average in size—five healthy Shih Tzu puppies. Each one weighs five to six ounces.

With the litter complete, return the puppies to the whelping box. Shu-Shu will push them into position so that they can feed. The touch and smell of her *teats* starts their mouths moving in strong sucking motions. Don't cuddle the puppies yet. The less you handle them, the better. After the puppies nurse, take Shu-Shu out to relieve herself. While she's gone, put fresh newspapers in the whelping box. It's a good time to call in the vet to check mother and pups.

If all goes well, your Shih Tzu puppies will grow rapidly. At ten days, the puppies' eyes will be open and they'll be able to hear. A few days later, they'll be standing on wobbly legs. Wagging tails and loud yapping mean they're hungry and want their mother. By two weeks, Shu-Shu's instinct is telling her it's time to begin *weaning* them. You can help by letting the puppies lick a mixture of milk, corn syrup, and egg yolk from your fingers. In a few more days, they'll be lapping milk from a bowl. By four weeks, the pups are eating from a bowl during the day and nursing only at night. They're cutting their baby teeth, and they'll chew on anything. By six weeks, they should be totally weaned.

A houseful of playful Shih Tzu puppies is a delight. When they're three to four months old, they're close to half their adult sizes. It's time to find new homes for them. With a good home and a little luck, each puppy can expect to live for another 12 to 15 years. One of them might go on to win Best of Breed at a dog show.

Shih Tzus come in all shapes and sizes!

SHOWING YOUR SHIH TZU IN COMPETITION

Sarah Whitley wanted to go to the beach, but Uncle Jack had other ideas. He dragged her to a dog show instead.

At first, Sarah didn't like the noisy, busy place. "It's smelly in here," she complained. "There are too many dogs!"

"That's what a dog show is all about," her uncle said with a smile. "This show is for all breeds, all ages, and all kinds of handlers. There's a class for puppies, and there's a class for first-time handlers. The big event is the Open Class. That's where the real champion of the show will be crowned."

Sarah thought about her own tiny Shih Tzu puppy. "I wonder what a champion Shih Tzu looks like?" she said. Uncle Jack led Sarah to the pens where the Shih Tzus were kept.

The row of beautiful dogs made Sarah gasp. Each Shih Tzu was perfectly groomed. Their hair was so long it almost touched the ground when they walked. The owners were fussing over the dogs, brushing each hair into place.

"My Nanjo could never look like that," Sarah said. "Five minutes after I groom him, he looks like a dusty, tangled mop."

"Showing a dog is hard work for both the dog and the owner," Jack told her. "Some owners won't put their Shih Tzus down on a thick carpet. If they do, the dogs will frazzle the ends of their hair as they walk."

Sarah admired a dog named Ch. Empress of Woodlawn. She decided that "Ch." must be short for "Champion."

"Could Nanjo ever be a champion?" she asked.

"Nanjo has a good pedigree," her uncle replied. "I think he has a chance. First, you have to prepare him for showing. Then, he has to win a total of 15 points at three different shows. If he does, you can call him Champion Sarah's Nanjo."

"Tell me what I have to do," Sarah demanded. She liked the idea of owning a champion Shih Tzu.

"First," Jack said, "you have to train him to behave at the show. Nanjo will have to stand quietly by your side, no matter what the other dogs do. When he's called for judging, he'll have to parade around the ring with his head high. Nanjo won't like it when the judge looks at his teeth, but he mustn't snarl. Your job is

During competition, Shih Tzus and their owners line up for the judges.

to show him at his best and to stay out of the judge's way."

Sarah was watching the Shih Tzus as they circled the ring. Each dog was a picture of perfect health and grooming. "I don't know if I can train and groom Nanjo that well," she said.

"You don't have to begin at the top," Jack assured her. "You can start by entering Nanjo in the Junior Showmanship division. In Novice A you'll be competing against children 10 to 12 years of age. Later, as you and Nanjo improve, you can move up to the open classes. That's where the adults compete."

Sarah clapped when the judge gave the blue ribbon to a silver-and-white Shih Tzu. "I know

Nanjo will be out there someday," she declared. "Thanks for bringing me to the show, Uncle Jack. As soon as I get home, I'll start training Nanjo for his first Junior Showmanship competition!"

WHY DOES A PUPPY CHEW UP THE HOUSE?

The whole family loved the new Shih Tzu puppy. Even cranky Uncle Ramon said Shenzi was the cutest dog he'd ever seen. Marcela took good care of the puppy and everyone was happy.

Sad to say, Shenzi and the Coronas didn't live happily ever after. When Shenzi was six months old, he began chewing. In one day, he chewed up a newspaper, one of Marcela's shoes, and little Joe's teddy bear. Mrs. Corona was so angry she swatted Shenzi with a broom. Marcela cried and Shenzi hid under the bed.

If the Coronas had done their homework, they'd have been ready for Shenzi's chewing.

All puppies go through this phase. When calm returned to the house that night, the family knew they had to do something. Mr. Corona smiled and said, "Being a Shih Tzu, Shenzi's mouth isn't very big. Think of how much damage a German shepherd could do! I talked to the breeder today, and she explained Shenzi's chewing problem."

Puppies chew for four reasons. First, they chew because they're curious and playful. Just like their wild cousins, they must explore everything around them. Chewing on things helps puppies learn about them. Second, chewing is part of teething. As the adult teeth break through, the puppy feels the need to chew on hard things. Eating soft, canned dog food makes the problem worse.

Third, teething comes during the "prehunting" phase of a puppy's life. In the wild, adult dogs bring chunks of meat back to the den. The puppies "attack" the meat as if it were live game. Shenzi attacked Marcela's shoe as if it were something his pack leader had left for him to chew on. Biting on the hard leather also made his gums feel better. Finally, puppies chew because they're bored or nervous. Left alone with no one to play with, they make up their own games. Chewing comes naturally to a Shih Tzu.

Shenzi's breeder gave Mr. Corona some tips on how to train the puppy. First, Shenzi has to earn his freedom. As long as he's destroying things, he must be confined. When he's free, someone should watch him. If he attacks a shoe or a toy, he must be corrected. Marcela should hold Shenzi by the collar while she shakes the shoe in his face. As she does this, she should say, "No, Shenzi, no!" in a commanding voice. Then she can give him his own chew toy. When he chews on it, she should praise him with a "Good dog!" and a loving pat.

Being firm and alert are the keys to breaking a bad habit. Like any puppy, Shenzi needs to know his pack leader is in charge. If Marcela corrects Shenzi one time and ignores his poor behavior another, he'll be confused. It also helps to give a puppy lots of exercise to burn off that extra energy. Marcela must set time aside each day for play and a long walk.

By being firm with your Shih Tzu, you can avoid the problems that the Coronas had. Shih Tzus are playful, fun-loving dogs. When they receive praise and discipline, they learn to behave well. And a well-behaved Shih Tzu can bring years of fun to you and your family.

▌GLOSSARY/INDEX

GLOSSARY/INDEX

Molars 15—The dog's back teeth, used for slicing and crushing.

Olfactory Patches 18—The nerve endings in the nose that provide a dog's keen sense of smell.

Pedigree 25, 41—A chart that lists a dog's ancestors.

Premolars 15—The dog's back teeth, used for slicing and chewing.

Puppy 6, 7, 23, 24, 25, 27, 28, 30, 31, 34, 35, 36, 37, 38, 39, 40, 43, 44, 45—A dog under one year of age.

Reinforcement 28, 30—Giving a dog a reward when it obeys a command.

Renal Dysplasia 24—A fatal kidney disease that Shih Tzus sometimes inherit from their parents.

Show Dog 24—A dog that meets the highest standards of its breed.

Stud Male 34, 35—A purebred male used for breeding.

Teats 38—The female dog's nipples. Puppies suck on the teats to get milk.

Umbilical Cord 37—The hollow tube that carries nutrients to the puppy while it's inside the mother's body.

GLOSSARY/INDEX